This Is My Story

by Frederick G. Frog

Lee Aucoin, *Creative Director*
Jamey Acosta, *Senior Editor*
Heidi Fiedler, *Editor*
Produced and designed by
Denise Ryan & Associates
Illustration © Samantha Paxton
Rachelle Cracchiolo, *Publisher*

Teacher Created Materials

5301 Oceanus Drive
Huntington Beach, CA 92649-1030
http://www.tcmpub.com
Paperback: ISBN: 978-1-4333-5484-7
Library Binding: ISBN: 978-1-4807-1140-2
© 2014 Teacher Created Materials

Written by James Reid
Illustrated by Samantha Paxton

Hi. I am Frederick G. Frog.

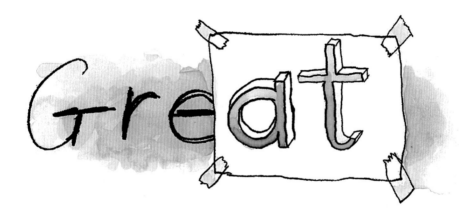

The G in my name stands for *Green,*
but I tell everyone it stands for *Great.*

I am the most amazing frog
in the forest.

I can jump farther than anyone.

I can croak louder than anyone.

I can catch bugs faster than anyone.

I can puff up larger than anyone.

I can climb higher than anyone.

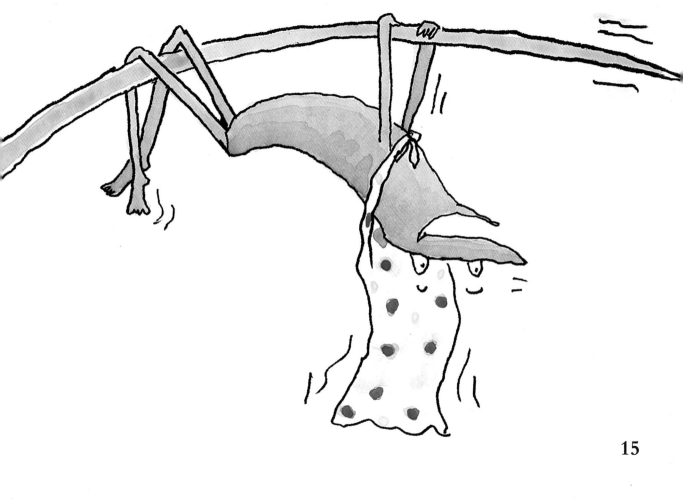

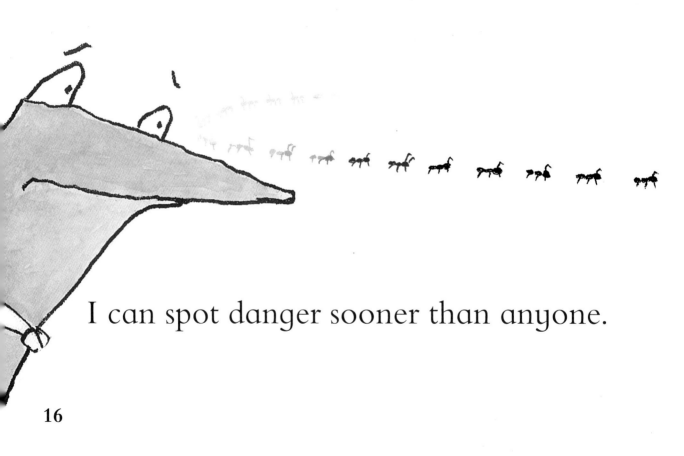

I can spot danger sooner than anyone.

I make more friends than anyone.

Hi. I am Frederick G. Frog.
The G stands for *Green*. Who are you?